What Kids Say About
Carole Marsh Mysteries . . .

I love the real locations! Reading the book always makes me want to go and visit them all on our next family vacation. My Mom says maybe, but I can't wait!

One day, I want to be a real kid in one of Ms. Marsh's mystery books. I think it would be fun, and I think I am a real character anyway. I filled out the application and sent it in and am keeping my fingers crossed!

History was not my favorite subject till I starting reading Carole Marsh Mysteries. Ms. Marsh really brings history to life. Also, she leaves room for the scary and fun.

I think Christina is so smart and brave. She is lucky to be in the mystery books because she gets to go to a lot of places. I always wonder just how much of the book is true and what is made up. Trying to figure that out is fun!

Grant is cool and funny! He makes me laugh a lot!!

I like that there are boys and girls in the story of different ages. Some mysteries I outgrow, but I can always find a favorite character to identify with in these books.

They are scary, but not too scary. They are funny. I learn a lot. There is always food which makes me hungry. I feel like I am there.

What Parents and Teachers Say About
Carole Marsh Mysteries . . .

I think kids love these books because they have such a wealth of detail. I know I learn a lot reading them! It's an engaging way to look at the history of any place or event. I always say I'm only going to read one chapter to the kids, but that never happens—it's always two or three, at least!
—Librarian

Reading the mystery and going on the field trip—Scavenger Hunt in hand—was the most fun our class ever had! It really brought the place and its history to life. They loved the real kids characters and all the humor. I loved seeing them learn that reading is an experience to enjoy!
—4th grade teacher

Carole Marsh is really on to something with these unique mysteries. They are so clever; kids want to read them all. The Teacher's Guides are chock full of activities, recipes, and additional fascinating information. My kids thought I was an expert on the subject—and with this tool, I felt like it!
—3rd grade teacher

My students loved writing their own Real Kids/Real Places mystery book! Ms. Marsh's reproducible guidelines are a real jewel. They learned about copyright and more & ended up with their own book they were so proud of!
—Reading/Writing Teacher

"The kids seem very realistic—my children seemed to relate to the characters. Also, it is educational by expanding their knowledge about the famous places in the books."

"They are what children like: mysteries and adventures with children they can relate to."

"Encourages reading for pleasure."

"This series is great. It can be used for reluctant readers, and as a history supplement."

The Mystery at

Dracula's Castle

Transylvania, Romania

by Carole Marsh

Published by Gallopade International/Carole Marsh Books. Printed in the
United States of America.

Managing Editor: Sherry Moss
Senior Editor: Janice Baker
Assistant Editor: Michael Kelly
Cover Design: Mark Mackey, Rightsyde Graphics
Content Design & Illustrations: Yvonne Ford

Cover Photo Credits: Jim Jurica, Jozsef Szasz-Fabian, Arne Thayson, ©Images from Photos.com
and istockphotos.com
Cover Illustrations Credits: Bob Faulkner, Brandon Laufenberg, Koson Kajeekailas, Guy-Paul
Michell-Dewlly

Gallopade International is introducing SAT words that kids need to know
in each new book that we publish. The SAT words are bold in
the story. Look for this special logo beside each word in the
glossary. Happy Learning!

Gallopade is proud to be a member and supporter of these educational
organizations and associations:

American Booksellers Association
American Library Association
International Reading Association
National Association for Gifted Children
The National School Supply and Equipment Association
The National Council for the Social Studies
Museum Store Association
Association of Partners for Public Lands
Association of Booksellers for Children

20 Years Ago . . .

As a mother and an author, one of the fondest periods of my life was when I decided to write mystery books for children. At this time (1979) kids were pretty much glued to the TV, something parents and teachers complained about the way they do about web surfing and blogging today.

I decided to set each mystery in a real place—a place kids could go and visit for themselves after reading the book. And I also used real children as characters. Usually a couple of my own children served as characters, and I had no trouble recruiting kids from the book's location to also be characters.

Also, I wanted all the kids—boys and girls of all ages—to participate in solving the mystery. And, I wanted kids to learn something as they read. Something about the history of the location. And I wanted the stories to be funny. That formula of real+scary+smart+fun served me well.

I love getting letters from teachers and parents who say they read the book with their class or child, then visited the historic site and saw all the places in the mystery for themselves. What's so great about that? What's great is that you and your children have an experience that bonds you together forever. Something you shared. Something you both cared about at the time. Something that crossed all age levels—a good story, a good scare, a good laugh!

20 years later,

Carole Marsh

Christina Mimi Papa Grant
"Mystery Girl"

Hey, kids! As you see—here we are ready to embark on another of our exciting Carole Marsh Mystery adventures! You know, in "real life," I keep very close tabs on Christina, Grant, and their friends when we travel. However, in the mystery books, they always seem to slip away from Papa and I so that they can try to solve the mystery on their own!

I hope you will go to www.carolemarshmysteries.com and apply to be a character in a future mystery book! Well, the *Mystery Girl* is all tuned up and ready for "take-off!"

Gotta go... Papa says so! Wonder what I've forgotten this time?

Happy "Armchair Travel" Reading,

Mimi

About the Characters

Christina, age 10: Mysterious things really do happen to her! Hobbies: soccer, Girl Scouts, anything crafty, hanging out with Mimi, and going on new adventures.

Grant, age 7: Always manages to fall off boats, back into cactuses, and find strange clues—even in real life! Hobbies: camping, baseball, computer games, math, and hanging out with Papa.

Mimi is Carole Marsh, children's book author and creator of Carole Marsh Mysteries, Around the World in 80 Mysteries, Three Amigos Mysteries, Baby's First Mysteries, and many others.

Papa is Bob Longmeyer, the author's real-life husband, who really does wear a tuxedo, cowboy boots and hat, fly an airplane, captain a boat, speak in a booming voice, and laugh a lot!

Travel around the world with Christina and Grant as they visit famous places in 80 countries, and experience the mysterious happenings that always seem to follow them!

Books in This Series

Table of Contents

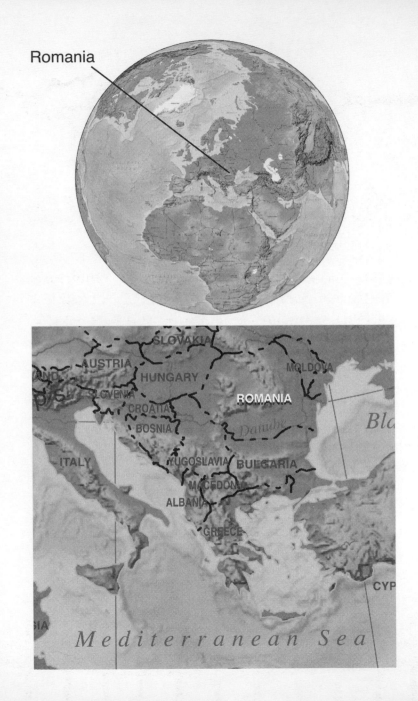

1

An Ad From Dad

Christina's and Grant's dad, Mike, sent their grandmother, Mimi, the famous children's mystery book writer, a small classified advertisement he clipped from the back of the Peachtree City, Georgia newspaper. It read:

CLASSIFIEDS

344

re Svc
er
27

an-
cat
ale.
72

47

ws

FOR SALE
One very large, very old castle. Once belonged to the famous Count Dracula. Needs some TLC. Great home for the fearless family. Call 1-800-VAMPIRE.

Homes
Unfurr

ELLF
cul
1-6

FAIF
ac
de

HAF
air
$75

HIF

It was just a joke—but not to Mimi. "Wow!" she said over a breakfast of blueberry pancakes one morning. "Count Dracula's famous castle is for sale!"

"Want to go take a look?" asked Papa, as he sloshed blueberry syrup over his scrambled eggs.

"Of course!" Mimi answered.

"Think Christina and Grant would like to go along?" Papa asked, pouring himself a large glass of tomato juice.

With a little smile, Mimi took the glass away from him and held it up to the light pouring in from the patio outside their sun porch.

With a gleam in her eye, Mimi said, "Vampires, blood, castles, history, mystery, legends, lore, gore...Oh, yes, I think our two mystery-loving grandchildren will be excited to go along on this trip."

Papa smiled. "You do know that this castle is just a little bit far away?"

Mimi smiled back. "The country of Romania," she said. "Transylvania, Romania, to be precise," she added.

She was surprised to see her cowboy/pilot husband shake his head back and forth. When he saw her puzzled expression, Papa said, in a deep, spooky voice,

"TRAAANSYLLLVAAANIA, my dear.

If you vant to go, pack your bags and call our grandchildren."

And Mimi did!

The Fearless Family

"What does TLC mean?" Christina asked, as they headed for Falcon Field and Papa's red and white airplane, the *Mystery Girl*.

"Tender Loving Care," Mimi explained.

Papa laughed. "It means that the place is a disaster and needs lots and lots of expensive work. I read somewhere on the Internet that the castle was built many centuries ago, so it's probably in bad shape."

"Who were the Teutonic Knights?" Grant asked.

"I don't know," Papa said. "We'll have to ask someone when we get there."

"Maybe it has rats!" Grant said.

Mimi and Christina squealed so loudly that Papa and Grant slapped their hands over their ears.

"Well, it's an old place," said Grant. "And since it's a castle, it probably has a dungeon, and dungeons always are wet and have rats—big ones!"

The girls squealed again.

"Pipe down," warned Papa. "Maybe it just needs some of that vampire blood washed off the walls."

Everyone got very quiet. "Not having second thoughts about going, are you?" Papa asked, smiling.

Mimi folded her arms across the front of her red jacket. "Absolutely not!" she said.

"Besides," said Christina, from the back seat of their SUV, "vampires are just make believe. Right, Papa?"

Papa did not answer. He turned into the airport entrance and waved at a fellow pilot.

"What does 'fearless family' mean?" Grant asked, re-reading the For Sale advertisement.

"It means you'd have to be very brave...or very stupid to buy the place," said Papa.

"Or both!" Mimi added, with a laugh.

"So, you're not really going to buy Dracula's Castle, right?" asked Christina.

"We're just going to look," Mimi said. "Just for fun."

"Or frights," said Papa, matter-of-factly.

Mimi punched her husband in the side. "Oh, quit scaring your grandchildren. We don't want them to chicken out."

"Hmmpf!" said Grant. "I'm not scared and I won't chicken out. A castle's just a big, old stone building. With lots of rooms. Maybe a few ghosts. Probably no electricity. Or bathrooms. Lots of spiders and roaches and..."

"Hush!" cried Mimi, as Papa pulled their car into a parking space. "Or I'll be the one to chicken out."

Christina and Grant laughed.

"Not you, Mimi," Christina said. "You're the mystery book writer. You're not scared of anything."

Papa chuckled as he opened the car door.

Mimi turned to look at her grandchildren.

"Well, I'm not scared of words on paper, but I'm not especially fond of, you know, creepy-crawly bugs. And the only mouse I like is on my computer."

"And Mickey," said Grant, a big Disney World fan. "Don't forget Mickey."

Mimi sighed. "And Mickey, of course."

"And you're not afraid of vampires?" Christina asked. It was a serious question.

Her grandmother tilted her head. "Hmm," she said. "I've never met one, so I don't know."

"I don't understand why the castle's owner would want to sell it," Grant said. "You would think that vampires would want to keep it in the family."

"Maybe they need the money," suggested Christina.

"Naw!" said Grant, shaking his head. "There's something more to this! I can feel it in my bones!"

Papa yanked open one of the back doors. "Are you guys going to help me with the luggage, or am I going to have to bite someone on the neck?"

Horrifica

"What are you reading, Grant?" Christina asked her brother. He held a book open with one hand and read as he tugged his wheeled suitcase with the other. This meant that he was constantly bumping into everything and everybody.

Grant turned the cover toward his sister and she read aloud, *"Encyclopedia Horrifica: The Terrifying TRUTH! About Vampires, Ghosts, Monsters, and More.* Gee, Grant, what kind of book is that?"

"A gooooooood one!" Grant said, never even looking up.

He rammed his luggage into a post.

"Watch where you're going," warned Papa.

"Before we need band aids!" Mimi pleaded.

Christina giggled. "Follow me," she told her brother. "Then you can pull and read."

Grant righted his suitcase and lined up behind his sister. He stood on the hot tarmac and continued to read as Papa and the others loaded the *Mystery Girl*. When he finally looked up, they were all in the plane, door closed, waving goodbye to him!

"Wait! Don't leave me!" Grant squealed. He peered up at the little red and white airplane, eyes squinting as if he were about to cry. "You need me!" he cried. "I have all the answers!" He waved his book at them.

With a grin, Papa reached back and opened the door. "We were just kidding," he said, tugging his grandson aboard.

"I'd never leave you behind," Mimi promised, blowing Grant a kiss. "But buckle up ASAP! The tower has cleared us for take-off."

As Papa revved the engine, and Mimi did the same front seat "backseat" driving she did whether Papa was driving a plane or a car, Christina and Grant settled in for take-off.

Over the whine of the engine, their grandparents did not hear the kids' discussion.

"What answers are you talking about, Grant?" Christina asked. "I didn't even know we had any questions."

Grant swiped at his sweaty bangs and his flushed cheeks grew even redder. "Of course we have questions!" he insisted.

"Like what?" Christina asked, truly puzzled.

Grant sighed. "Like, are vampires real? Do they really drink your blood? Was Dracula real? Did he really live in this castle Mimi's taking us to look at? Are we spending the night there? Will we be safe? And why would they want to sell the castle or is there something else going on?"

Christina slunk back into her seat and began to perspire, too. "Gosh, Grant, you're right. I never thought about any of this being real. You know how Mimi is...always making stuff up to entertain us."

Her brother nodded. "Yeah," he agreed, "but you also know she's a history nut. And a lot of this stuff is history."

"And legend, too," his sister reminded him.

"Yeah," said Grant, as the *Mystery Girl's* nose lifted off the runway in a gentle motion, followed by the wheels. They were suddenly airborne, with the pine forests of Peachtree City soon fading to small green dots in the background. "But what's real and what's not? That's what we need to know."

Christina pointed to the book. "And you think the answers are in there?"

Grant sighed. "I think so, but I think this is one mystery trip where we might not know what—or even who—to believe."

Christina nodded. "Then we'll have to be extra vigilant," she warned.

"*Vampire* vigilant!" Grant insisted.

"*Verrry* vampire vigilant!" his sister agreed.

"WHAT?" cried Papa back to them. "You say you're very hungry? But we just left!"

Both kids began to giggle. Fortunately their grandfather could not hear them well over the sound of the *Mystery Girl's* beating propeller. They gave him a thumbs-down to indicate that was not what they had said. However, they didn't volunteer what they had been talking about, and Papa went back to flying the plane.

Soon, Christina and Grant settled back to read the book together. By the time they landed in New York City to catch a transcontinental flight to Transylvania, they both were one thing: TERRIFIED!

4

A Mysterious Man

It was hot, humid, and sunny when they landed at New York's LaGuardia Airport. While Papa got the *Mystery Girl* squared away in a hangar until their return, Mimi, Christina, and Grant headed into the icy-cool terminal to find their gate and get some lunch.

"Pizza!" cried Grant, immediately spotting a small, red-checkered café.

"You always want pizza before we travel," Mimi complained with a groan. "Just what I need before I fly—pizza pie."

But Mimi could never refuse her grandchildren's goofy grins or other twist-her-arm antics. This time it was Grant, on bended knee, palms pressed together in the air as he intoned, "Oh, please, oh please, wonderful grandmother, pizza pie or we will cry."

Passersby stared. Mimi relented. "Enough, already, Grant! I surrender. Get in line. I'll have pepperoni."

Instantly, Grant stood up and hopped into line. Christina followed. By the time their grandmother had found a table near the large windows overlooking the runways, the kids showed up with a large pepperoni pizza, sodas, and a stack of napkins.

"Change?" Mimi reminded them. The kids groaned and forked over a few bills and some coins. "Nice try," their grandmother said.

"How will Papa find us?" Christina asked, tucking a napkin into her shirt collar.

Mimi pointed to Grant. "We'll be the ones with a kid that looks like a hungry vampire!" After one bite, Grant's mouth was encircled—nose to chin to dimples—in red pizza sauce.

"I vant to drink your blood!" Grant intoned.

Mimi gave him "the look" that meant settle down and behave yourself. Grant shrugged and grabbed another slice of pizza.

"Seriously, Mimi," Christina said, plucking a piece of pizza from the pie and sliding it to her paper plate. "What interests you so much about this castle that's for sale?"

Mimi gave her granddaughter a probing look. It was her "I can figure out any mystery" stare. When Christina finally blinked, Mimi chuckled.

"Sooooo," said Mimi. "Can I deduce that you two are a little scared of visiting Dracula's Castle?"

The children's ducked-head silence told her the truth.

"But what if vampires are real?" asked Grant. "Vat if they vant to drink OUR blood?"

"That's silly!" said Christina.

"You read the book!" her brother reminded her.

"What book?" asked Mimi.

Grant tugged a book from his backpack but it wasn't the book that he had been reading earlier.

This one was entitled, *VAMPYRE: The Terrifying Lost Journal of Dr. Cornelius Van Helsing.*

"Grant!" said Christina. "Didn't you bring anything to read besides vampire books?"

"He has more?" Mimi asked, a worried look on her face.

"Don't ask!" Christina said. Grant just smiled meekly.

Mimi grew serious. "Look, you two, knock off all this vampire stuff. It's fun to think about and talk about, but really, Romania's a lovely country—you'll see. All this Dracula stuff is just folklore, you know, not true."

Grant got very quiet and nibbled at his pizza. Finally, he said softly, "Mimi?"

"Yes, Grant?" said his grandmother.

"Uh," said Grant, "I think you might be wrong."

Mimi reared back with a startled look on her face. She never thought she was wrong! "What?"

"Really," said Grant, apologetically. "I think there really was a Count Dracula. And he really might have been a vampire."

Christina, quiet, zipped her head back and forth, listening.

Mimi frowned. "Grant, I want this trip to be fun, not scary."

Her grandson looked doubtful.

Suddenly, Papa appeared. He had a big grin on his face and a strange-looking man in tow. "Hey, you guys," he said. "Meet Mr. Van Helsing. He can tell us all about Dracula and vampires!"

"See," Grant said softly.

Mimi just stared and stared with her big green eyes. She looked pretty frightened herself!

Air Dracula

Mr. Van Helsing was traveling on the same flight to Transylvania. "Welcome to Air Dracula!" he joked as they all boarded the big British Airways jet. Mimi frowned.

Mimi and Papa sat by the windows, and Grant, Christina, and Mr. Van Helsing sat together in the center section of seats. The kids scrambled to sit on each side of the interesting gentleman.

While Mimi strained to hear what was being said, the roar of the jet blasting through the air at over 400 miles an hour prevented that, so the children were able to enjoy Mr. Van Helsing's version of the famous Dracula story.

"You see," he began, as the plane left the runway and hoisted itself into the sky, "there are many myths about the legend of the **malevolent** man known as Count Dracula."

Just hearing the man's strange accent say the words, *COOOUNT DRRRRACULA* gave Christina and Grant cold chills up and down their backbones resting against the padded airline seats. What an unexpected adventure, they both thought and grinned at one another across the man's arms folded across his chest.

"Some people believe that the fictional vampire in the famous Dracula book is based on a real man named Dracula," Mr. Van Helsing continued. "In the Romanian language, Dracula means 'the son of Dracul.' And, indeed, Vlad Tepes Dracula was the man's name!"

"So Dracula was real?" squealed Christina softly in surprise.

"Vlad Tepes Dracula was a real man born in 1431," Mr. Van Helsing corrected. "Dracula was the main character in a novel by Bram Stoker."

Grant looked confused. "Well, tell us about the real Mr. Dracula, please."

Mr. Van Helsing nodded. "Vlad Dracula's father was a prince. One day, Dracula and his younger brother were kidnapped by the father's enemies and held in captivity for six years. This did not give him a very happy childhood."

"I should think not!" said Christina with a frown. How frightening, she thought, to be captured and held hostage away from your family.

"And," added Mr. Van Helsing, "Dracula was even more upset to learn that his father had been murdered, as had his older brother."

"Yikes!" said Grant. "People sure were mean back then!"

Mr. Van Helsing nodded. "It was a harsh time."

"So what did Dracula do next?" Christina bravely asked.

To their surprise, Mr. Van Helsing bent his head low and whispered, as if only for them to hear, "He was an angry man. He set out to get revenge, and he never stopped. You could say blood flowed over the land. He killed many people and made his prisoners build a fortress. These ruins today are known as Castle Dracula."

"And that's where we're going?" Grant asked, his voice trembling. Before he could answer, a flight attendant leaned over and asked them, "What would you like to drink?"

Grant looked up with his big, blue eyes. "Anything," he said, "but tomato juice!"

Because they were flying across the time zones, dinner was soon served and it began to get dark. Mr. Van Helsing spotted an old acquaintance at the rear of the plane, and got up to talk with him. Soon, Grant and Christina had fallen across his seat and gone to sleep, each dreaming rather frightful dreams of spooky castles and mysterious men.

Welcome to Bucharest

It was dark when they landed at the airport. In fact, it was the middle of the night. Grant and Christina had a hard time waking up. Rubbing their eyes, they staggered down the aisle tugging their wheeled suitcases.

"Are we in Hungary?" Grant overheard a passenger ask.

"I'm hungry," Grant mumbled, rubbing his tummy.

"We're in Bucharest," Grant heard Mimi answer the passenger.

"I didn't get any rest at all," grumbled Grant.

At night, most airports look the same, Christina thought as they deplaned the aircraft.

The black tarmac glistened with rain. The blue and red colors of the taxi and runway lights blurred in the mist like smeared paint.

"You can sleep in the taxi," Mimi said gently, giving both children a hug. That hug was the last thing they remembered until morning.

"Wow!" said Christina, waking up in the hotel and rubbing her eyes. "I must have slept like a zombie."

"Wrong country, sister," Grant said, hopping out of bed. "Vampire, you slept like a vampire."

"Don't start!" Mimi warned from their doorway. "I don't want to hear so much of that vampire talk. There's a lot more to Romania than Dracula, so just knock it off or I'll be in trouble with your parents for scaring you."

Grant giggled. "Nothing scares me!" he swore, jumping on the bed and making a cape of his pajama top.

Christina shook her head. "Some things scare me," she admitted. "Like all that stuff Mr. Van Helsing told us last night...oops!" she added, with a sly look at her grandmother.

Mimi stamped her foot and shook her blond curls. "I just knew I should have sat with you two! What did that man tell you?" She looked worried.

"Nothing much," Christina promised. "Just a little history."

"Yeah," added Grant. "Really old history. Was there really a year 14-something?"

Mimi laughed. "Yes, Grant, there was, and quite a few years before that, too. Get dressed now, and let's go meet Papa for breakfast."

As their grandmother turned to leave the room, Grant winked at his sister. "Old history and bloody history!" he whispered.

Mimi spun around. "What did you say, Grant?"

Grant looked stunned. He didn't want to upset his grandmother. "Uh, mud...muddy...I think my shoes got muddy in the rain at the airport last night." He shook his bare foot and Christina giggled.

Mimi just looked puzzled and said, "Well, hurry up. Papa's already downstairs. We need to get to Transylvania, you know, and meet the real estate agent."

Grant gave Mimi a serious stare. "Are you sure he's real?" he asked. "Is he fiction or non-fiction?"

Mimi shook her head. "Grant, I have no idea what you're talking about! All I know is that he's a she and she'll be waiting on us and I don't like to make people wait so don't make me wait because Papa is waiting...downstairs, now."

Christina popped out of bed. "We're up, Mimi, promise! We'll be right there. Just go on ahead. Grant and I will catch up in a minute."

Her grandmother smiled, nodded, and left the room.

"What was that all about?" Grant asked, as soon as Mimi was out of listening range.

Christina grinned. "It was about this," she said and pulled a copy of *Dracula* by Bram Stoker out from under her pillow!

7

Roaming Around Romania

As it turned out, the real estate agent was in the dining room with Papa.

"I was already here in town for a meeting," Ms. Alucard explained, as she repositioned the big, dark wraparound sunglasses on her rather thin nose.

"She was just telling me about the castle," Papa added, as Mimi and the children took their seats. "It sounds like quite a place!"

Mimi looked surprised at Papa's enthusiasm. He often humored her mystery larks. She just couldn't figure out his sudden interest in a creepy, overpriced, distant castle...unless, she thought, it was because Ms. Alucard was so pretty!

"Quite unique, **eloquent**, and romantic!" the real estate agent swooned. "An heir of Romania's former royal family currently owns what everyone calls Dracula's Castle." She turned serious and whispered. "The sellers want a buyer who will respect the property and its history, of course."

Grant looked puzzled. "You mean not scrub the blood off the walls?"

"Grant!" Mimi cried. "Please eat your food. I believe you told me you were starving last night when we got off the plane."

"Yes," added Papa. "Eat your *ou* and drink your *lapte*."

"Huh?" said Christina.

"Your eggs and your milk," Ms. Alucard translated merrily.

"Ou-kay," Grant said, hesitantly. "Hey, Christina, put your napkin in your lapte, would you?"

Mimi just shook her head and nodded for the real estate agent to continue.

"The asking price starts at a mere $40 million," Ms. Alucard announced simply, as if that was completely reasonable, perhaps even a bargain. "But, we have several interested buyers. So, I believe the actual selling price will be closer to $135 million. After all, it's one of a kind, you know!"

"No doubt," said Mimi, sipping her coffee.

"Does the castle have an intercom system?" Grant asked, milk dripping down each corner of his mouth. Mimi frowned at him. She could never tell when he was serious or when he was about to pull a fast one on all of them.

Ms. Alucard tilted her head with a thoughtful look. "I don't believe so," she said. "It does have a telephone system, but I'm sure an intercom could be installed. But what would be the purpose?"

Papa shook his head. He knew the woman should have never asked.

"So you can make announcements throughout the castle, of course," said Grant, matter-of-factly. But his sister was already starting to giggle. "You know, like, DRACULA, DINNER IS NOW SERVED IN THE DINING ROOM!"

While the others couldn't help but laugh at Grant's silliness, the real estate agent just grimaced. It was clear that she didn't have much of a sense of humor when it came to small children.

Therefore, it only made sense that Grant would continue. "Or, hey, Drackie, be a good vampire, and brush your fangs before you go to the dungeon and get in your coffin!"

Guests at other tables were now staring at the curious Americans who seemed to be having so much fun at breakfast. They looked puzzled, but perhaps a little jealous.

"Okay, Grant," said Mimi, dabbing at her eyes with her napkin. "That's enough. We get your point." She turned to Ms. Alucard. "Our arrangement was to spend the weekend at the castle. Does that still apply?"

"Of course," the real estate agent answered. She stared down her nose at the children. "And will they be coming along for the weekend?"

Papa understood her meaning. He reared his shoulders back and straightened up, tucking the local newspaper he had been reading under his arm with a slap. "Oh, yes, indeed," he said. "We wouldn't think of buying a $135 million dollar castle without their approval. They're our heirs, you know?"

Ms. Alucard stared at her lap, and then said through a forced smile, "Naturally! I'll get the car. Our train to Transylvania leaves at dusk!"

As she left the table and paraded haughtily through the restaurant, Papa and the kids snickered. But Mimi frowned. "Hey, you guys, be nice. We are guests in this country. Let's not be rude, even to rude people."

"Yeah," said Grant, hopping up. "Let's be nice to everyone. If I see Dracula, I'm gonna kiss him."

"Sure," said Christina with a giggle. "What you'll do is run like a big scaredy cat."

Grant turned and gave his family a very curious, serious stare. "No, I won't," he said quietly. "You don't understand. I've read the books. I know how to handle these vampires. Just watch." He turned back around and stalked off to **wallow** in his own thoughts.

"Hmmm," said Mimi, always able to sense when one of her grandchildren was upset. "Perhaps he does."

"Well," said Papa, picking up the check. "You never know what skills will come in handy in a foreign country."

He and Mimi followed Grant.

When Christina did not follow, he turned around and said, "Coming, Christina?"

But his granddaughter was staring out into a far hallway, deep in thought. Quickly, she spun around and joined her grandparents. "Yes," she said. "I just thought I saw someone I know."

She did not look happy. Not happy at all. In fact, she looked rather pale, as if she'd seen a ghost.

8

A Train to Transylvania

Bright streaks of lightning crisscrossed the night sky outside the speeding train. The brilliant flashes bounced off the low clouds, lighting up the nooks and crannies of the woods and mountains outside Grant's window. He marveled at the bizarre patterns the tiny rain droplets made as they streamed horizontally along the window.

"Did you see that?" Christina asked, looking out the window over Grant.

"See what?" asked Grant.

"I don't know, but I'm pretty sure I saw something move out there during that last flash of lightning," Christina said, sliding closer to Grant.

Grant adjusted his focus from the window's glass to the area beyond the streaking rain and waited for another bolt of lightning to light up the sky.

"That was a big one," thought Grant, as the lightning **illuminated** the countryside. "I see it!" Grant almost shouted. "It's a bat!"

Lightning crackled repeatedly, and Grant and Christina followed the bat's progress as it raced alongside the train.

"That's a really big bat," Christina said. "Not like the little brown bats we have back home in Peachtree City."

"Yeah," Grant said. "It's a vampire bat." He raised his hands into claws and turned toward his sister. He had stuffed two white triangular pieces of cardboard in his mouth to look like fangs.

"AHH!" Christina screamed.

Mimi looked over at Papa, who was still fast asleep. "You two quiet down or you might wake the dead," she said.

"Okay, Mimi," said Christina. She punched her brother in the arm. "Don't ever scare me like that again!"

"All right! All right!" Grant said through giggles, trying to hold in his laughter.

Christina pointed at the bat outside the window. It had flown within three feet of Grant's window. Grant looked at the bat just as it turned briefly to face him. Lightning lit up the sky around the bat, as its mouth opened in a frightful snarl, revealing two pointed canine teeth. Grant and Christina jumped back in their seats.

As the bat glared at them, it flapped its wings faster, pulling itself ahead of Grant's window. Grant lost sight of the bat at the point where the two train cars met. He thought for sure he saw it turn in between the train cars.

Grant and Christina kept their eyes on the door that separated the train cars. They expected to see the bat fly between the two cars and off to the left side of the train. They both gasped when the train door flew open in a single motion. Ms. Alucard stood between the two cars. She quickly snapped her sunglasses over her dark eyes and entered the car.

As she walked down the aisle past them, she didn't glance their way. "Did you see that?" asked Christina.

"Yeah!" Grant said. "In fact, that's the freakiest thing I've seen since Mimi—"

"Are you children okay?" Ms. Alucard snarled, as she stood in the aisle slightly behind their seats. "You both look like you've seen a ghost."

"Uh, no!" Grant said. Just a vampire, he thought.

"Good!" said Ms. Alucard. "Because we will be arriving in Brasov shortly." She turned to talk to Mimi who was writing down ideas for a new mystery book.

"I didn't see her get on the train when we boarded," Christina whispered. "Did you?"

Grant shook his head. "Not until a minute ago," he replied, looking at the door separating the two train cars. The vampire bat was nowhere to be seen.

Chilly Castle

"It's really dark out here," Christina said, gazing at the canopy of clouds overhead that were occasionally lit by bursts of lightning. The pounding rain had stopped before they had arrived at the train station in Brasov, but the clouds looked like they were going to open up again soon.

As their long black limousine climbed the mountainside to the castle, lightning crackled above the treetops, backlighting the castle and its towering turrets.

"Wow!" Grant said. "Isn't that the coolest thing you've ever seen?"

"No!" said Christina. "It's kind of scary looking."

The castle stood like a solitary soldier at the top of the mountain. Its base was surrounded by trees, which the howling wind whipped into a frenzy. Christina wondered how the leaves managed to stay on the branches.

"Oh, my!" said Mimi, craning her neck to look at the castle's turrets. "I didn't know the castle was this big!"

"Wait until you get inside," Ms. Alucard said. "You will be amazed at the size of the rooms and the beautiful furnishings."

"I'm sure I will be," Mimi said.

Grant and Christina jumped out of the limo just before it came to a complete stop at the rock staircase leading up to the castle entrance. As their feet hit the ground, the clouds opened up, and buckets of rain poured down on them.

"Hurry up, Papa and Mimi," Christina shouted, "or you'll get soaked."

"We're right behind you!" shouted Papa, as he ran hand in hand with Mimi up the stairs toward the castle's towering entrance. Mimi's red hat almost blew off as a gust of wind threatened to carry it down into the valley below, but she grabbed it and held on tightly.

Chilly Castle

When Christina reached the top of the stairs, she turned around and saw Ms. Alucard. She was standing in front of the limo, staring upward into the falling rain with her sunglasses on and a half-opened black umbrella in her hand.

With every flash of lightning, Christina could see the limo and Ms. Alucard's images merge to form a single silhouette. It looked like a bat with its wings spread! Ms. Alucard slowly climbed the stairs toward the tower entrance. When she reached the dimly lit archway, she snapped off her sunglasses.

Grant and Christina gasped at the sight of her dark brown eyes outlined in thick black eyeliner.

"Welcome to Bran Castle!" Christina jumped at the sound of the deep voice behind her. "My name is Hermann von Salza. I am the houseman of Bran Castle."

Papa stuck out his hand and gave von Salza a hearty handshake. "Glad to meet you," Papa said. "This is quite a place you have here."

"It contains a lot of Romanian history," von Salza said, shaking the hands of all his guests.

"But the hour is late, and I'm sure you are tired and ready for a good night's sleep. We will talk more about the castle tomorrow when I give you a tour."

Von Salza did not shake Ms. Alucard's hand. "Ms. Alucard," he said. "I will take it from here."

"They are all yours," Ms. Alucard remarked, turning toward Mimi and Papa. "I will be back on Monday morning to pick you up. We can discuss whether you want to buy the castle at that time."

A chilly breeze tingled Mimi's spine, and she tightened her jacket as she turned to face Ms. Alucard. "It's chilly in here," Mimi said, as the group turned to follow von Salza up the steep staircase to the first floor.

As Ms. Alucard turned to leave, she stepped back into the entranceway shadows and put her sunglasses back on. She looked back over her shoulder at Grant and Christina, who were still staring at her. When she smiled at them, light glimmered off the two pointed canine teeth on either side of her mouth.

Grant and Christina ran up the staircase after their grandparents.

Queen Maria

Grant followed Christina up the staircase behind von Salza, Mimi, and Papa. The lighting was brighter on the first floor. Von Salza seemed much taller and thinner than he had downstairs. Grant also noticed that his black hair was combed back flat and came to a V-shaped point at the front.

Von Salza was telling Mimi about the different rooms on the floor. "These rooms are decorated in Renaissance and Gothic styles," he explained. "The Passing room has a large stone fireplace and two handcrafted Renaissance chests from the sixteenth century. The Gothic room, which connects to the Passing room through a pinewood-sculptured door, also has a stone fireplace where several pieces of gothic art are displayed. The gothic furniture is from the fourteenth century.

"I took the liberty of adding an extra bed to this room for your grandchildren," he continued, opening the door to a spacious, magnificent chamber decorated in blue and gold. "They will be staying in Queen Maria's bedroom."

"Who's Queen Maria?" Christina asked, as she entered the room with Mimi.

"She was a member of the Romanian royal family who lived in the castle before World War II," Grant said.

"Well done, young man," said von Salza. "You seem to know something about our castle."

"He likes to read," Christina said.

"I know that until the queen moved in," Grant said, "Bran was a real castle stronghold and not a summer palace. She was the one who foo-fooed up the castle with electricity, running water, and telephones."

"Ahh, I see," von Salza said. "You were hoping for a manly castle like in the days of yore, where knights did battle to save the maiden in distress."

"Yeah!" Grant said. "Something like that."

"You sound a lot like my son, John," von Salza said. "He doesn't like how fancy, or 'foo-fooed,' as you say, the castle is, either." He heard footsteps echoing off the stone floor in the hall outside the room. "In fact, I think that's him now."

A boy about the same age as Grant strolled into the room. A younger girl was right behind him.

"Who sounds a lot like me, Father?" John asked.

"I do," Grant said. "Hi, my name's Grant, and this is my sister Christina and my grandparents. We call them Papa and Mimi. You can, too."

"Hello," John said. "I'm John, and this is my sister, Maria."

"Maria—just like the queen who lived in this castle?" Mimi asked.

"Yes," Maria said, as she curtsied. "Father named me after Queen Maria."

"That's lovely," Mimi said. "Do you live in the castle?"

"Yes," Maria said, "on the floor above this

one. We have grown up in the castle and know everything about it."

"Even stuff about Count Dracula?" Christina asked.

"Especially stuff about Count Dracula," John said. "If it were not for tourists wanting to see or hear as much as possible about Count Dracula and vampires, Bran Castle would probably be in ruins."

John turned to his father. "Father, our chores are done, can we show Grant and Christina around?"

"Yes," von Salza said. His eyebrows rose. "But behave yourselves."

"Yes, Father," John replied.

After the children left the room, von Salza turned toward the large bed along one side of the room. "This hand-sculptured column bed was made in the eighteenth century out of several types of wood. It was given to Queen Maria by Romanian actress Nicoleta Volescu and was sculptured for the Italian Baroque period.

"And now," he continued, "I will leave and let you retire for the evening."

"Thank you so much," said Mimi. "I am very tired!" She gladly closed the door behind von Salza.

Mimi lugged her red suitcase into the

This house is a dangerous place for foreigners!

bathroom. Something in the sink caught her eye. "What is that?" she asked softly.

"Papa!" Mimi cried.

Dungeons and Other Scary Things

Suddenly, I felt a hand on my shoulder, and heard the Count's voice saying to me, 'Good morning.' I started, for it amazed me that I had not seen him, since the reflection of the glass covered the whole room behind me...

Christina laid in the dark in the Passing room reading *Dracula* and listening to the sounds of the castle at night. The wind was rushing around the castle rooftops, porticos, and other odd angles of the castle's construction, causing spooky sounds from a low-pitched groan to a screeching whistle.

Christina had pulled the bed covers over her head as she laid belly down on the mattress. The book lay open in front of her with her flashlight shining upon its old wrinkled pages. She just couldn't go to sleep, so she continued reading,

...In starting I had cut myself slightly, but did not notice it at the moment. Having answered the Count's salutation, I turned to the glass again to see how I had been mistaken. This time there could be no error, for the man was close to me, and I could see him over my shoulder. But there was no reflection of him in the mirror!

CRREEEEEEK!

A low groan came from somewhere in the castle. Christina pulled her blanket tighter over her. That was definitely not the sound of the wind!

The sound was closer. Christina flicked off her flashlight. Suddenly, she felt something on the side of her leg. It moved up slowly, inch by inch, like a large spider climbing a log. She started to shake, but knew she had to face whatever it was.

Spinning around, she whipped her blanket down and slapped at her leg. Her hand hit something smooth and larger than she expected, and then the scariest face she'd ever seen appeared inches away from hers. She opened her mouth to scream, but a hand covered it.

"Christina," Grant whispered, giggling as he pulled the flashlight away from under his face. "Be quiet! As Mimi says, you might wake the dead. Especially in an old castle like this."

"Grant!" Christina shouted. "You're going to get it, just you wait and see!"

"I'm sorry," Grant said, still giggling. "I couldn't sleep, so I thought you might want to take a look around the castle with me to see if we can find the dungeon."

Christina kicked off her blanket and leaped out of bed. She was still dressed. "I was wondering when you were going to suggest that," she remarked, shoving her sneakers on her feet and tying the laces tight. "But didn't you say the castle was built on rock, so there was no dungeon?"

"Yep," Grant said, "but I've read that one of the towers was used as a jail or a type of dungeon. We just have to find the tower."

"Okay," Christina said, grabbing a flashlight from her luggage on the floor. "I'm right behind you."

"Cool," Grant said. "There's a connecting door from my room into the room John called a saloon. Let's see how close that gets us to the staircase so we don't have to cross the whole hallway."

Within just a few seconds, they were in the saloon. "I don't know why they call it the saloon," Christina said. "It doesn't look like the ones in those old Westerns Papa watches."

"Yeah!" Grant said. "I get the feeling that the word 'saloon' means something different to them, like it does on a cruise ship."

"How did we get from a castle in the middle of Transylvania to a cruise ship?" Christina asked.

Grant shook his head. "Cruise ships have a large room, called a saloon, where passengers relax and socialize," he said. "I think that's what this saloon is for."

"Oh," said Christina. "Aren't you the expert! But, I see what you mean." She shined her light on a portrait of a soldier on one side of the fireplace. The eyes on the portrait were mesmerizing. They almost looked real.

"Whoa," Grant said. "Check out this fireplace." He walked into the hearth. The area where the wood burned was bigger than both of them. "Can you imagine the size fire they would have had going in this fireplace back then? Come on in here." Grant stepped to the back of the fireplace and leaned against the back wall as he pointed his flashlight up the chimney.

"Sorry," Christina said, as she walked toward the opening of the fireplace. "I make it a habit not to climb into firepla—." She tripped over a raised stone in the hearth and fell forward. She reached out and grabbed a small metal dragonhead, which stuck out from the side of the fireplace, to break her fall. Just for a second, she noticed the dark cross on the dragon's head. There was a matching dragonhead on the other side of the fireplace, but there was no cross on its head.

As her weight hit the dragonhead, she twisted her body to bring her feet back under her, and the dragonhead turned in her hands. She heard a scraping sound and turned toward Grant just in time to see him fall backwards as the rear wall of the fireplace hearth opened inward.

I Vant to Suck Your Blood!

"Wow!" Grant shouted, as he stuck his head back through the hole at the back of the fireplace. "That was cool. How did you do that?"

"I tripped," Christina said, pointing at the dragonhead. "I grabbed for the dragonhead and it turned. Are you okay?"

"Yeah," Grant said. "There's a set of stairs in here. Follow me."

Before Christina stepped into the fireplace, she looked up at the portrait on the wall. The eyes looked vacant, not like the eyes she had seen a minute ago. She noticed that there were three crosses in a triangular pattern on the back fireplace wall. The staircase was dusty smelling, but bone dry.

"I hate spider webs!" Christina screeched as she walked into a sticky **labyrinth**.

Grant saw her flailing around at the webs. "Hold still," he said. "I'll get them off of you." After pulling most of the web from his sister's hair, his flashlight beam landed on the top of her head, where a big spider sat staring into the light. He quickly brushed it off without saying a word. She owes me for that one, Grant thought. "Okay, you're all clean," he said. "Next time— look where you're going!"

Christina let out the breath she had been holding. "Are you sure there are no spiders on me?" she asked.

Grant flicked his flashlight beam all around her. "Yeah," he said. "You're clean as a whistle. Now, let's get going."

Christina moved slowly up the stairs after Grant, flashing her light from side to side and up and down. She was breathing heavily by the time they reached the landing.

"There's nothing here," Grant said, as he looked at the blank walls on the landing. "No dragonheads to turn or anything. It must be a dead end. We just wasted our time."

Christina looked at the walls closely. "Hmm," she said. "Maybe not. See this darker-colored brick? There's a cross on it, just like the one on the dragon head at the entrance to the fireplace." She pointed at the cross and pushed in on it.

SCREEEEECH!

The kids heard the sound of stone scraping against stone once again, and turned to see an opening appear in the wall.

"This is really getting to be fun," Grant said, as he crawled through the opening. "I'm lucky I have such a smart sister!"

"You sure are," Christina said. The children popped through the back wall of another fireplace into a massive room with old furniture pushed along the sides of the walls. The center of the room was empty, like a dance hall.

"I'll bet this is where the queen held her fancy balls," Christina observed. Her voice echoed around the room. "I guess that staircase would come in handy if you needed to get away from someone."

"Yeah," Grant said, running around the room to peek into every corner. "I wonder where the dungeon tower might be."

"It is this way," a voice said.

Grant looked at his sister. "You didn't say that, did you?" he asked.

"No!" Christina said in a high-pitched whisper.

"I can take you to the dungeon tower," the voice said. "I am very familiar with it. I spent several weeks there in my youth."

"Ahh!" Grant stuttered, "who...who are you?"

"I am Count Dracula," the voice replied. A figure in a black cloak seemed to float at them through the darkness. His black eyes were unmoving as they stared straight at Grant and Christina. A red liquid dripped down his chin from two large fangs that protruded from his open mouth.

"I vant to suck your blood!"

shouted the count.

"RUN!" Christina yelled, as she twirled around and ran to the fireplace staircase.

Instead of running, Grant reached into his back pants pocket and pulled out a silver cross. He held it up in front of him. "You can't hurt us," he said, his jaw set in determination. "I command you to back off."

But Dracula kept coming.

Will the Real Dracula Please Stand Up?

As Christina was about to duck through the fireplace entrance, she saw the three crosses in the shape of a triangle on the back of the fireplace wall, just like the one downstairs. No time to think about that now, she thought. I'm getting out of here!

Suddenly, laughter broke out behind her. Christina stopped and looked back. John and Maria emerged from behind Count Dracula, pulling up the cloak to reveal a rolling platform. John fell to the floor, grabbing his stomach and roaring with laughter.

Christina saw her brother standing firm, only ten feet from Dracula. He slowly brought down the silver cross he had been holding up high. He began to giggle, then broke into a belly laugh.

"We are sorry we scared you," Maria said, giggling, as she reached for Christina's hand.

"Yeah," John said, between giggles. "We are sorry, but you should have seen the look on your faces, especially you, Christina. I wish I had a camera."

John leaned on hands and knees, still trying to control his laughter. He looked up at Grant. "I thought that you would have wet your pants, like some of the other Americans we have pulled this on. But you didn't back down! I do not know that I would have been able to do that in the face of Dracula."

"I haven't wet my pants since I was one year old," Grant said. "All I can say is—I wish I had thought of it first! That was cool! It looked so real."

Grant climbed on the platform and pulled the Dracula mask off the helmeted head perched on a shiny coat of armor. It still had the red "blood" on it. "Ketchup?" he asked.

"No," John said. "Tomato paste mixed with a smidgen of milk. It looks more realistic and runs like blood."

"Cool!" Grant said.

"Are you okay, Christina?" asked Maria.

"Yes," Christina said. "I'm just trying to get my heart to stop racing. This is the second time tonight that I've been scared." She scowled at Grant. "I hope there won't be a third."

"So," John said. "Do you want to see the dungeon tower where Count Dracula was kept prisoner for two weeks?"

"Prisoner?" Christina said. "I thought this was Count Dracula's castle."

"No," Maria said, "the real Castle Dracula is in ruins. But because of Count Dracula's internment here at Bran Castle and the famous novel about a vampire named Dracula living here, Bran Castle has become known as Dracula's Castle."

"So," Christina said, "you're saying that Count Dracula is not the same person as the vampire Dracula."

"Correct," said Maria. "Bram Stoker, the writer of the first Dracula book, just used Count Dracula, or Vlad Tepes Dracula, as the model for his Dracula vampire in the book."

"Okay," said Grant, moving his eyebrows up and down. "So, where is this dungeon?"

"Follow me," John said. "It is not far."

Everyone lined up behind John, and like a withering snake, followed him in and out of rooms, along balconies, and down stairs until they reached the ground level overlooking the cliff the castle was built on. John opened the massive door leading into the dungeon tower and led them down the stairs in total darkness, except for the light from Grant and Christina's flashlights.

At the bottom of the stairs, they entered a rectangular chamber. Christina's hand slid around the corner of the staircase, brushing over an old dirty mirror, as her flashlight illuminated three coffin-like chests. Each had a single black

Will the Real Dracula Please Stand Up?

The Mystery at Dracula's Castle

cross on them. They sat on tables arranged in a triangle. Christina's light moved on to the lower section of the darkly stained walls. "Is...is that blood?" she asked.

"Yes!" said John. "Blood that is centuries old. Remember, this castle was used as a battle station for war. Many prisoners lost their lives in this dungeon."

"Are you sure the blood isn't from Dracula's victims?" Christina asked.

"We told you, Count Dracula was not really a vamp—" John was interrupted by a noise coming from one of the three chests arranged in a triangle. A loud tapping sound came from one of them. When the chest started to wiggle , all four of the children backed up.

Grant exclaimed, looking at John. "How did you do that?"

"I didn't...I did not," John said, with a frightened look on his face, as he pressed himself up against the back wall of the dungeon tower.

Leave My Dwelling at Once!

Maria wrapped her arms around John. "What is going on, John?" she said, as the chest started to vibrate more violently.

"I do not know!" John screamed over the noise. "It's not me. I do not know what is doing it."

The chest's vibrations caused a heavy wrought iron candlestick on the table to topple over. It fell toward Christina. Grant dove toward his sister, knocking her clear of the falling candlestick. Her flashlight fell from her hand, smashing into pieces on the floor. Grant and

Christina landed on the staircase leading out of the dungeon tower.

"AAAHHHHHHHHH!"

Grant heard Maria scream. The chest lid was slowly opening! A wrinkled hand suddenly slid out from under the lid, ready to shove it open the rest of the way.

Grant grabbed a metal torch from its holder on the wall in case he needed a weapon.

The chest suddenly stopped moving. "Why are you disturbing my sleep?" a loud, raspy voice said. The withered hand caressed the edge of the chest's lid.

Grant looked over to find John in the darkness. John and Maria were gone! There was no hole in the wall or anything. They were just gone!

Christina screamed when the chest lid flew open and a bone-thin man rose from its dark interior. The look in his eyes was mesmerizing. Just like the portrait, Christina thought.

Grant tossed the torch aside and reached into his back pocket again. He jerked the silver cross free just as the man snarled loudly, "You are not welcome here! Leave my dwelling at once and never return!"

The man saw the cross and took a step forward. "Leave! Leave now, before I forget my manners!" he screamed again.

Christina grabbed Grant by the arm. "Let's go!" she shouted. As she yanked Grant up the staircase, she glanced into the mirror and saw the man standing with his hands on his hips.

She and Grant raced up the staircase, never looking back.

When they cleared the tower, they flew up another set of stairs, and raced through several rooms and hallways back to Grant's room. Panting, they locked and braced the door with chairs, pillows, suitcases, shoes—whatever they could grab. They jumped under the covers of Grant's bed, glancing anxiously at the door until they finally drifted off to sleep.

Neither of them had seen the note flutter off their door and land under Grant's bed. It said,

I say again, leave my dwelling and do not return!

We've Been Vamboozled!

A loud knocking at the door caused Grant and Christina to jump out of bed. "Grant, is Christina in there with you?" Papa asked.

Grant pushed the pile of debris away from the door. "Yes!" he shouted, as he unlocked and opened the door.

"What in the world are you two up to?" Papa asked, seeing the mess near the door. "Did you have a bad dream or something?" he asked, looking at Christina.

"The 'or something' is about right," Christina said. "How is Mimi this morning?" she asked, trying to change the subject.

"She's okay," said Papa. He and Mimi had decided not to tell the kids about the note they'd found. "You both slept so late you missed the tour of the castle by Mr. von Salza. This here is one heck of a castle. Your grandmother found a perfect place to write in one of the towers and I've found some interesting reading in the queen's library. But you two need to get ready, because we are going on a tour of Brasov."

"Okay," Grant said. "We'll be down as fast as we can."

"Fine," said Papa. "Your grandmother's in a rush because she's got some great ideas for a new book she wants to get started on this afternoon. We'll be waiting for you downstairs. Oh, von Salza's two children will be joining us."

After Papa left, Grant closed the door. "How are you doing?" he asked.

"I'm okay," Christina said, smiling. "I'm worried about John and Maria. They really looked frightened when they fell through the hole in the wall. I've been wondering if they got away okay. It's sounds like they did."

"What hole in the wall?" Grant said. "I didn't see any hole."

"When you grabbed the torch out of its holder," Christina said, "the wall behind them opened up, they fell through it, and then the wall closed up!"

"I wish you had told me that last night," Grant said. "I couldn't figure out how they got out of the room."

"I really couldn't talk last night," Christina said. "That...that vampire thing was scary!"

"Yeah," Grant said. "I've been thinking about that. I think we've been vamboozled, and not by John this time!"

Go Home!

After a quick tour of the castle's courtyard, their guide, Sir Arthur Bradenburg, president of the Brasov town council, herded the group into two separate limousines for the ride back to Brasov. The four children took one, and the three adults took the other.

"We were hoping you made it out of there okay," John said. "I saw you on the stairs and figured you could make a run for it."

"We did, but not until we saw the vampire thing," Grant said.

"But there is no such thing as a vampire," said John.

"Exactly," Grant said, as he told them what had happened after they fell through the hole.

"Where did that hole lead to, anyway?" Grant asked.

"To a set of stairs that led up to the castle kitchen," John said. "We decided to go back to our rooms before our father found us missing. He doesn't really like us to roam the castle at night."

"I can understand why," Christina said, "when you have vampire things crawling out of old wooden boxes."

"He wasn't a vampire," Grant said.

"How do you know?" asked Maria.

"It's easy," Grant said. "When I showed him my silver cross and shined my flashlight in his eyes, it didn't even bother him. According to vampire lore, the cross should have repelled him and the light should have blinded him."

Christina almost jumped out of her seat. "You're right!" she shouted. "I just remembered something. I saw the vampire's reflection in the mirror on the wall in the dungeon tower. He couldn't have been a vampire, or I wouldn't have seen his reflection."

"Okay," John said. "But besides me, who would want to scare you guys or us? And for what reason?"

"Good question," Grant said. "Last night I kept asking myself the same question, and then the words of that guy came back to me. He said, "You are not welcome here,' and 'Leave my dwelling at once!"

"Yeah," Christina said. "Just before we left, he shouted, 'Leave! Leave now, before I forget my manners!' He definitely needed to work on his people skills. He was quite rude!"

"Guys!" Grant said. "Someone doesn't want Mimi and Papa to buy this hunk of rock!"

Here, Kitty, Kitty

"Bran Castle was originally built as a stronghold in 1212 by the Teutonic Knights," Sir Arthur Bradenburg said, as the group strolled down one of the oldest merchant streets in Brasov. A horse-drawn cart lumbered by, piled high with cabbages. An old couple with scarf-covered heads sat in the driver's seat. Past the lively street market and vendors, lush, hilly pastures were nestled among the Carpathian Mountains.

"Who were the Teutonic Knights?" Papa asked.

"Have you ever heard of the Templars?" asked Bradenberg.

"Yes," Papa said. "They were a military group of knights, back around 1200 AD, that fought in the Crusades, which were fought by European Christians trying to retake portions of the Holy Land previously captured by Muslim forces."

"Exactly," Bradenberg said. "The Teutonic Knights were another group of knighted soldiers authorized by the church to fight battles and to protect European travelers to the Holy Land. You could tell them apart from the Templars by the large black cross they had on their surcoats. They fought proudly during all of the Crusades. Now, there are no descendants of the original knights left. But the order continues as a small group in Vienna, Austria that does charity work."

Grant began to get bored with Bradenburg's stories. "Hey, John," he said. "Do you know if you're descended from knights?"

"Not that I know of," John said. "But wouldn't that be cool?"

"Yeah!" Grant said. "But your name would sound better than mine."

"Really," said John. "How so?"

"Sir John," Grant said, "sounds more knightish than Sir Grant."

"You have a point there," John said.

"Hey," Christina said. "You knights of the geek table, isn't that Ms. Alucard in that store over there?"

"It sure is," Grant said. "Let's go see what she's doing." The children pressed their noses against the store window.

"She's just talking to the guy behind the counter and petting a cat," Maria said.

"That woman scares me," Christina remarked. "There's something strange about her. Don't you think so, Grant?"

"Yep," Grant answered. "If there really are vampires, she has got to be one."

Just as Grant said that, Ms. Alucard ducked her head toward the cat, and then jerked it back. She turned to face the window with the cat hanging loosely in her hands. Red-tinged fangs hung from Ms. Alucard's mouth, as she hissed at the children.

They turned to run, but ran smack into Papa, Mimi, and Bradenberg.

"What's going on?" Mimi asked, seeing the frightened looks on Grant's and Christina's faces.

All of the children were pointing at the store window, when suddenly, Ms. Alucard walked out, holding a beautiful black cat and a small shopping bag.

"Ms. Alucard," Mimi said, "are you out shopping today?"

"As a matter of fact, I am," Ms. Alucard said, looking at the children. "I needed to pick up some party favors for a party my husband and I are having tonight. I thought these might be fun for the guests to wear." She pulled a pair of red-tinged fangs out of her bag, stuck them in her mouth, and hissed. "I vant to suck your blood."

Christina and Grant breathed a sigh of relief. They wearily slid into the back seat of the limo.

Grant's hand ran across a piece of paper in the seat. "What's this?" he asked Christina. She leaned over to read it with her brother.

Go back home to America! This castle will never be your home!

Who doesn't want us here? Christina wondered.

Here I Come, Ready or Not

The two limousines pulled up to the castle entrance. "I enjoyed showing you around our little town," Bradenberg said. "If there's anything else I can do, please don't hesitate to call." Bradenberg shook Papa's hand and kissed the back of Mimi's hand. As he pulled his hand away and got back in the limo, Christina noticed the shiny gold ring on his finger. It had a black cross on a white background.

"Mimi," Grant said, "can we play outside for a while?"

Mimi looked over at Papa, who gave a slight nod. "Okay," she said. "But Mr. von Salza said dinner will be ready in about..." Mimi looked at her watch. "In about an hour. So, be back inside by then."

"We will," Christina shouted, as she ran to join the other three kids.

John led them around the west side of the castle into the forest. The long shadows cast by the late afternoon sun highlighted the specks of pollen and other dust particles floating in the cool air. John led them to the remains of a building with bright green moss covering its northern surfaces.

"What was this?" Grant asked.

"I do not really know," said John. "But it must not have been very important if nobody took the time to maintain it. Do you guys want to play tag?"

"That sounds like fun," Christina said. "I'll be 'It'." Christina ducked her head, covered her eyes, and started counting. When she reached ten, she opened her eyes. "Watch out," she said. "Ready or not, here I come!"

Out of the corner of her eye, Christina saw movement behind a tree and slowly crept over to it. Just before she got there, Grant jumped out and ran back to the castle.

John had popped out from another tree, but stopped short when he and Christina both saw Grant suddenly disappear! "What was that?" Christina cried. "The ground just opened up and swallowed him!"

19

Woman's Intuition

Grant gazed at the sky through the opening above him. "I'm okay," he said to himself, patting his skinny body from head to toe.

"Grant!" Christina shouted. "Are you okay?"

"Yeah," Grant said, his voice echoing. "I'm fine!" He saw three faces staring down at him. "Don't get too close to the edge of the hole, or it may–" Before he could finish, the ground beneath Christina and his friends gave way. All three of them tumbled through the hole, now even larger.

"I know that you guys were missing me, but I really didn't expect you to join me down here," Grant said, as they all stood and rubbed the dirt off their clothes.

"That's not funny," Christina said. "We could have gotten hurt. Oh, my!" Christina was looking over Grant's shoulder. A big black cross on a white background was etched into a pillar of stone behind Grant's back.

He followed everyone's gaze and turned to face the pillar. "That's the crest of the Teutonic Knights," Grant said.

"Uh, huh!" said Christina. "Just before he left, I saw the same crest on Sir Bradenberg's ring. And remember the same cross, which I thought was an X, that led us into the room where we met John and Maria?"

"Whoa," John said. "You mean to say that Bradenberg is a Teutonic Knight? That is incredible. We have known him all our lives. He comes over and plays chess with our father and he has never mentioned that he is a Teutonic Knight."

"Didn't the 'Sir' part of his name give you a clue that he might be a knight?" asked Grant.

"Of course, we knew he was a knight," John said. "But we thought he was a descendant of the Romanian royal family, not the Teutonic Knights that built this castle."

"Well," Grant said, "as Mimi likes to say, 'It's good to learn something new every day.' Now, we need to learn how to get out of here."

"Hey," Maria said. "Do you think that tunnel may lead us anywhere?"

Grant looked down the dark tunnel. "Hmm," he said. "It's going in the right direction back toward the castle. I'd say we try it."

"That's great," Christina said. "But aren't you forgetting that we have no flashlights?"

Grant reached into his pocket and pulled out a small penlight. "A Boy Scout is always prepared," he said, wiggling the penlight back and forth.

"You're not a Boy Scout!" Christina said.

"True," said Grant. "But I'm always prepared. Let's go."

Grant took the lead. He moved slowly and pointed out puddles, spider webs, and other obstacles in their way.

Christina knocked a spider web to the side. "Why do I always let you get me into these situations?" she asked.

"It's because Mimi says you have to watch out for me," Grant said. "And the fact that you love your little brother."

"Huh!" Christina said. "Brothers!"

"I know what you mean," said Maria.

"What's this?" John asked, running his hand along the rough tunnel wall. "Shine your light over here."

Grant moved the light beam around the tunnel toward John. The beam landed on stones similar to the ones that formed the foundation of the castle. As they walked further up the tunnel, the floor evened out, the air became less heavy, and the musty odor seemed less offensive.

When the kids reached the end of the tunnel shaft, they had to make a choice—right or left.

"Okay," Grant said. 'Let's vote. Right or left!"

"I say we go right," John said.

"No," Maria said. "I think we should go left.

"I agree with Maria," Christina added.

"What do you think, Grant?" John asked, figuring Grant would vote with him.

"Hmm," Grant said. "I think we should go to the right."

"All right!" John said.

"But," Grant added, "Papa says a man should never go against a woman's intuition. So I vote left."

"There's hope for you yet," Christina said.

John looked disappointed.

"It's okay, John," Grant said. "If they're wrong, we'll turn around and take your tunnel. Let's go or we'll be late for dinner."

They had only traveled 20 feet when the tunnel abruptly ended at a staircase leading upward.

Grant handed the penlight to Christina. "You always seem to know how to find your way through solid walls," he said. "Lead the way."

When they reached the top of the stairs, Christina examined the smooth, rectangular rocks. They were all the same color, with smooth textures, and they all had mortar plastered evenly around them. But nothing stood out as a lever or something to push.

Christina looked closer. "Aha!" she cried. A tiny, black Teutonic cross was barely visible in the corner of the lowest brick. She pushed on the rock's center, but it didn't budge. Then she tried pushing on the cross itself. The corner of the rock moved inward, and the children heard the mechanical sound of gears grinding.

"Here we go," Grant said.

A door-sized portion of the wall popped open a couple of inches. Together, they pushed it far enough out so they could squeeze through one by one. Then they quickly pushed it shut.

"Where are we?" Grant asked.

"We're in the castle's courtyard near the back wall of the chapel," John replied.

Grant turned toward John. "That is why I always...well, almost always, listen to Papa, cause he's always right." Grant looked at his watch. "Hey, we made it back in time for dinner."

John shook his head. "Woman's intuition, huh?"

Knights of the Teutonic Order

The next morning, Grant and Christina were up early. They had slept soundly after their adventurous day, and were ready to explore the forest tunnels once again.

"Well," Papa said, watching them gulp down their breakfast. "You guys are sure raring to go. What's the rush?"

"We're just going to play with John and Maria," Grant said.

"Have you and Mimi made up your minds about buying the castle yet?" Christina asked.

"No, not exactly," Papa said, pushing his cowboy hat up. "Your grandmother loves the tower where she's been writing and I like everything else about the castle, but strange things keep happening."

"Strange things?" Grant said. "Like what?"

"Well," Papa started, "I'll take a book from the library with me to another room, set it down, do something else, and then go back to the book, and it's not where I left it. Then I go back to the library and it's in the exact same spot where I got it in the first place. Mimi says the same thing has been happening to her." He stopped short of telling the kids about the note.

"Are you sure that Mr. von Salza isn't putting the stuff back?" Grant asked.

"Yes," Papa said. "I asked him and he said he wasn't. It's just all pretty strange. Anyway, I'm off to the library again to finish a book on the Teutonic Knights. Funny thing though, Bradenberg said there were no surviving descendants of the original Teutonic Knights. But, according to this book, one family survived and its descendants are here today, but their identity is being kept a secret by the order's current members."

Grant and Christina looked at each other. "I wonder who that could be," Grant said, smiling secretively at Christina.

"Mimi thinks it's Sir Bradenberg," Papa said.

Christina gasped. "Why would she think that?" she asked.

"She saw a Teutonic black cross on his ring when he kissed her hand goodbye," Papa said.

"Oh!" Christina said. "Is it okay if we go and play with John and Maria? They're supposed to meet us in the courtyard."

"Yeah," Papa said. "Be back in time for lunch. Mimi wants to tour the countryside after we eat."

"Okay," Grant said. "Sounds like fun."

Grant and Christina skipped out into the hallway and disappeared down the stairs.

I wonder what they're up to, Papa thought. He headed back to the library and settled in an overstuffed chair with his book on the Teutonic Knights. As he opened it to the bookmarked page where he had left off, a handwritten note stared back at him.

The Meeting Place

The tunnels seemed darker than Grant remembered, even with his bigger and brighter flashlight. John and Maria had also brought their flashlights. They started down the tunnel that led away from the hole they had fallen through yesterday.

"Do you think there's anything down here, John?" Grant asked.

"No, not really," John said. "But I love to explore. Maybe we will get lucky and find a sword or something that the knights left behind."

"That would be cool," Grant said. "But I was thinking it would be great if we could find old documents that told about the knights." Grant went on to tell John and Maria about the book that Papa was reading. "What if we could prove that Sir Bradenberg is the lone surviving descendant of the original Teutonic Knights? We would be among only a handful of people that know the truth, and probably the only non-Teutonic Order members."

"Mimi always says you have a big imagination," Christina said, as they followed the tunnel around a bend.

"Stop!" Maria said. They all stopped and turned to look at her.

A low whistling sound came up the tunnel.

"What's that?" Christina whispered.

"It sounds like wind blowing through a hole," Grant said. Suddenly, a thought came to him and he ran his flashlight around the tunnel.

"What are you doing?" John asked.

"I just realized something," Grant said.

"What?" asked Christina.

"Have you noticed how clean the tunnel is?" Grant asked. "Even the staircase is clean. There are no spider webs or rocks to stumble over like in the other section of tunnel."

"Yeah," Christina said. "So what?"

"Have you ever heard of entropy?" Grant said. "It means that everything wears out, breaks down, grows old, or falls apart unless it is maintained. Someone has been maintaining this tunnel, which means we are not the only people who have been down here recently."

"We should go back," Maria said.

"No way," Grant, John, and Christina said at the same time. "We're here, let's see what we can find," Christina said.

"Yeah," Grant said. "As Mimi says, 'never quit something you've started.' Follow me."

They trudged down the long tunnel until they found another offshoot tunnel with some light coming from the end of it.

"Let's go this way," Grant said, slipping down the new tunnel. For a minute, he felt like a bug flying toward one of those electronic bug zappers.

The end of the tunnel opened into a dim chamber lit by torchlight. "Oh, my," Christina said, gazing at a massive, round wooden table in the middle of the room surrounded by ten huge chairs.

"Now, this is really cool," Grant said, as he scanned the walls of the chamber.

"I've never seen anything like this," Christina said. Three large banners featuring the Teutonic cross hung from the ceiling in a triangle. Four other banners hung along the outer walls from ceiling to floor with phrases written in what she thought was Latin. Unfortunately, she couldn't read Latin.

"I wonder what those say," Grant said, looking past Christina at the banners.

"I do, too," Christina said. "I also wonder why they hung the three banners with the crosses in a triangle instead of along a wall. It makes them hard to see." Shiny golden goblets sat on the table in front of each chair. The wall at the back of the chamber showed a faded image of the original Teutonic Knights in a battle. It looked centuries old.

Footsteps sounded down the tunnel leading to the chamber. The children froze.

The Mystery at Dracula's Castle

Hide!

"Hide," Grant mouthed, and pulled Maria behind one of the banners. John followed Grant's lead as he and Christina ducked behind another banner just as a man entered the chamber.

The bone-thin man filled each of the goblets with a purple liquid. Christina peeked out from behind the banner and gasped. She quickly slapped her hand over her mouth.

The man finished his pouring and left the chamber. When his footsteps faded into the distance, Grant and Maria, and John and Christina emerged from behind the banners.

"That was—"

"I don't—"

"The gardener—"

"Vampire—"

They all tried to speak at the same time. Christina put her hand up. "Hold it," she said. "Everyone gets a turn. Me first. That was the vampire thing we saw in the dungeon tower and I've seen his eyes in several of the castle portraits. He's been watching us."

"He is the castle gardener," Maria said. "I have never heard him speak to anyone."

"I hate to interrupt," Grant said, "but his filling up the goblets is probably a sign that they're about to have some sort of meeting. We need to get out of here."

The tunnel echoed with the sound of footsteps.

"Hide behind those banners and be quiet!" Grant whispered, as he and Christina jumped behind a banner to the left of the faded wall painting.

Hide!

Christina was facing the chamber wall and the large faded painting. She was afraid of turning around and making noise, so she remained perfectly still, staring at the images of three courageous knights swinging their swords in ancient battle.

Eleven men filed into the chamber. Sir Arthur Bradenberg led the group around the table. All, except for the gardener, who stood by the entrance, took positions behind a chair.

Sir Bradenberg spoke in Latin for a minute and then grabbed his goblet and raised it high. The other nine men did the same.

"I call this meeting of the Teutonic Order," Bradenberg called, took a drink from his goblet, set it back on the table, and sat down.

"First order of business?" Bradenberg asked.

An older man spoke up. "Sir Arthur," the man said, "it is the same as last time. We all feel that it is time for you to come out of hiding. The world needs to know that you are the rightful owner of this castle before someone like that couple from America buys it. Once it gets out of

Romanian hands, it will be extremely hard for you to reclaim it."

"You are the only descendant of the men who built Bran Castle. It rightfully belongs to you," another man added.

"I understand what you are all saying, but now is not the right time," Bradenberg said. "We do not have the money it would take to maintain the castle as I wish. That is why the royal family wants to sell it. They do not even have the money to make the necessary improvements."

"My only purpose for going public with my identity is so I—we—can take care of this historic castle. And our only chance to take care of the castle is to find the hidden Teutonic treasury, which my ancestors concealed somewhere in the walls of the castle for just such a purpose. Without it, the castle will fall into disarray or someone else will take possession of it."

He turned to the short gentleman on his right. "Bela, have you had any luck in solving the only clue we have to the treasury's whereabouts?" he asked.

Hide!

Bela shook his head. "All of us have tried everything we know to solve the riddle," he said, glancing at the four banners, "but as of this moment, we have nothing."

"Then all is lost to us," Bradenberg said. "I will take my secret to my grave."

A Simple Child, A Simple Riddle

Bradenberg looked at each of the four banners with their Latin phrases. "How could my ancestors have left us a riddle so simple-sounding that is so hard to solve?" He read the words in English,

Dare not search the castle high,
For fortunes there do not lie,
Search three crosses of battles past,
And find the swords to fortunes vast.

Bradenburg shook his head again. "I don't know what else we can do, my brothers!" he exclaimed.

Christina tried her best not to move. Her focus was on the large wall painting. "Battles past..." she thought, as she looked at the knights swinging their swords. "Search the cross..." All of the knights had a cross on their surcoats. Suddenly, her eyes widened as she looked at the area of the painting in the center of the knights.

The first man to speak looked at the bald gardener. "How goes your search and have you gotten rid of the family that is interested in the castle?"

"I have had no luck, either," the gardener said. "No sooner do I think I have solved the riddle, than I discover I was wrong. As far as the family, I do not believe they are truly interested in buying the castle. The woman is a writer and her only interest seems to be in writing and not the castle, although her husband appears to be enjoying the books in the library."

"My only regret is scaring the children—" the gardener started.

"I hope you did not hurt them," Bradenberg said.

"No," the gardened replied. "But I am afraid that I may have scared the girl beyond—"

Christina jumped out from behind the banner. "You didn't scare me," she said. Several of the men leaped to their feet.

"What!" Bradenberg couldn't believe his eyes. A child was in their sacred chambers! "How did you get in here?" he asked, his eyes ablaze.

Grant slid out from behind the banner and stood next to his sister. John and Maria followed. A gasp went through the room.

"We're sorry," Christina said, "but we found the tunnel system by accident."

"They know your secret," Bela exclaimed. "They must not be able to leave here!"

"Good going, sis," Grant said.

Christina walked over to Bradenberg. "Would you let us go if I show you the answer to your riddle?" she asked. "After all, the world should know who truly owns Dracula's castle."

Bradenberg shook his head. "As you have heard, nobody has been able to solve the riddle. What makes you think you can when they haven't been able to?"

"That's easy," Christina said. "I've been staring at the answer since we hid in this chamber. To solve the riddle you need to be in this chamber. The first two lines of the riddle are telling you not to waste your time searching the castle for the treasury. The third and fourth lines tell you where you'll find the treasury."

"Sir Arthur," the old man said. "This is preposterous. A simple child cannot solve this riddle.

"A simple child," Bradenberg mumbled, "a simple riddle. Go on, tell me more."

Cross Your Heart

"As I said, I can't tell you, I have to show you." Christina walked over to the painting on the wall. "You said the third line of the riddle was, 'Search three crosses of battles past,'" she said. "There are three crosses hanging in this room and three crosses on the knights in this painting. They both form triangles."

Grant knew Christina had solved the riddle. He had never seen her more confident.

"Grant, can you lend me a finger?" Christina asked. She put her two forefingers on two of the crosses and Grant put his on the third. "Push," she said.

As soon as they pushed inward on the crosses, mechanical sounds could be heard coming from behind the chamber wall, but nothing happened.

Christina moved to the side of the painting. "Tell me the last line of the riddle again," she said.

"'And find the swords to fortunes vast,'" Bradenberg said, watching Christina closely. His eyes followed her finger to the center of the triangle formed by the three fighting knights. A pile of swords laid on the ground. Christina's finger pointed to the center of the pile. Where the swords crossed each other, they formed another Teutonic cross. Christina pushed on the cross and more mechanical sounds emanated from the wall.

Suddenly, the portion of the wall with the painting on it separated in two and swung inward. Christina removed a torch from its holder and walked into the opening, lighting up a chamber filled with shimmering gold coins and glittering jewels.

"I give you the Teutonic treasury!" she said.

"ᒪᓄᕼᓇᒪᓇᒪᓇᒪᓇᒪᓇᒪᓇᒪᓇᒪᓇ?"

Grant, John, and Maria exclaimed.

25

A Promise is a Promise

"Grant, did you and Christina tell Mimi or Papa what happened?" John asked, as he watched his father load suitcases into the limo.

"We sure did," Grant replied. "They were really proud of Christina for figuring out the riddle. And we all promised Sir Bradenburg, just like you and Maria did, that we would keep his secret until the time is right for him to announce it. So, until he does, our lips are sealed." Grant made the motion of zipping his lips and throwing away the key.

Christina and Maria walked up behind the boys, busily trading home and e-mail addresses so they could keep in touch.

"Well, say your goodbyes and get in the limo," Papa said. "I get the feeling Mimi's going to want to make a quick getaway." He glanced at Mimi talking with Ms. Alucard, who didn't look very happy.

Grant and Christina had just climbed into the limo when Mimi jumped in. She let out a big sigh. "Driver, let's go," she said. "I am sooooo ready to go home!"

Grant looked out the window at Ms. Alucard. She stood, motionless, with her hands on her hips and her dark eyeglasses shielding her from the sunlight.

"Are we buying the castle?" Christina asked, already knowing the answer.

"No way," Mimi said. "I've decided that a beach house may suit us better than a drafty old castle!"

"Sounds good to me!" Grant agreed. "But what I think you're really saying is that the castle scares you," he added. "I think you're afraid there might still be vampires there."

"Grant," Mimi said, lowering her sunglasses and peering at Grant over the top of them, "I've told you there are no real vampires. They were created by a writer to frighten people. That's all!"

As the limo sped down the mountain away from the castle, Grant looked out the rear window to where Ms. Alucard had been standing. She wasn't there. Suddenly, a large vampire bat appeared in the window behind the limo. Grant could swear that it looked at Mimi and hissed.

"I don't know," said Grant. "I just don't know."

The End

About the Author

Carole Marsh is an author and publisher who has written many works of fiction and non-fiction for young readers. She travels throughout the United States and around the world to research her books. In 1979 Carole Marsh was named Communicator of the Year for her corporate communications work with major national and international corporations.

Marsh is the founder and CEO of Gallopade International, established in 1979. Today, Gallopade International is widely recognized as a leading source of educational materials for every state and many countries. Marsh and Gallopade were recipients of the 2004 Teachers' Choice Award. Marsh has written more than 50 Carole Marsh Mysteries™. In 2007, she was named Georgia Author of the year. Years ago, her children, Michele and Michael, were the original characters in her mystery books. Today, they continue the Carole Marsh Books tradition by working at Gallopade. By adding grandchildren Grant and Christina as new mystery characters, she has continued the tradition for a third generation.

Ms. Marsh welcomes correspondence from her readers. You can e-mail her at fancub@gallopade.com, visit the carolemarshmysteries.com website, or write to her in care of Gallopade International, P.O. Box 2779, Peachtree City, Georgia, 30269 USA.

Built-In Book Club

Talk About It!

1. Would you like it if your parents wanted to buy a castle similar to the one in the book? Why or why not?

2. How would you feel if someone played a trick on you like John and Maria played on Grant and Christina?

3. Why do you think bats kept appearing every time Ms. Alucard arrived?

4. Sir Bradenburg wants to preserve the castle because of its history. Why is it important to preserve historical buildings and artifacts?

5. Would you like to travel to Romania

someday? Why or why not?

6. Christina and Grant spent time reading scary vampire stories. What type of stories do you like to read before bed?

7. What was your favorite part of the book? Why?

8. The children travel on the *Mystery Girl* and on a commercial airline jet in this book. Have you ever flown in a small plane? Have you ever traveled on an airline jet? What do you think some of the differences would be?

Built-In Book Club

Bring it to Life!

1. Map It! Find a map of Europe on the Internet. Ask several book club members to draw a map of Europe and label the countries. Color Romania in a special color and decorate it in a special way—maybe with little bats! List Romania's neighbors.

2. Draw it! Name it! Draw a medieval castle like Bran Castle. You might want to draw it at night, with the moon shining bright and a few bats circling around! Then, name your castle. Be creative, be inventive, be spoooooooky!!

3.   What time is it, really, and what's the weather? Use Internet tools to help you find out the time difference between your home state and Romania.   Decide what time it is in Romania compared to the time in your town!   Then, decide what the weather would be in Romania today compared to where you live.

4. Make a Teutonic Knight shield! Look for images of the Teutonic Knights on the Internet. Then, find a large cardboard box. Cut the side off the box, and make your own Teutonic Knight shield out of the cardboard. Remember to make a handle on the inside so you can hold it in front of you for protection!

5.   Travel to Transylvania! Transylvania is a beautiful and interesting place! Divide into three groups to research Transylvania. One group can research the area's history, another group can research the area's geography, and the last group can research the area's people and how they live. Prepare reports on posters to present to the book club. Be sure to add lots of pictures!

Transylvania Trivia

1. The name 'Transylvania' means, "land beyond the forest."

2. Transylvania is a province in the country of Romania. It is located in the Carpathian Mountains.

3. Transylvania is a beautiful place, featuring tall mountain peaks, deep valleys, caverns, and crystal-clear streams and waterfalls.

4. Peasants still drive horse-drawn carts and cut the grass with sickles and scythes in much of Transylvania.

5. The Transylvania countryside is dotted with beautiful buildings, including ancient wooden churches, monasteries painted inside and out with Biblical scenes, and majestic castles.

6. Transylvania offers some of the best snow skiing in Romania!

7. Transylvania has many ancient "walled" cities with fortresses and towers, built as defense against invading armies.

Glossary

dwelling: housing that someone is living in

 eloquent: expressing yourself clearly

gothic: something belonging to the Middle Ages, or a style of architecture popular in Europe from the 12th to the 16th centuries

 illuminate: to make something visible or bright with light, or to bring something to light

internment: the act of confining someone in a prison or similar place

 labyrinth: a complex system of paths or tunnels in which it is easy to get lost

Glossary

 malevolent: evil, or having an evil or harmful influence

mesmerize: to fascinate someone or absorb all of someone's attention

silhouette: a dark outline on a light background

snarl: to growl in threatening manner

surcoat: long, flowing garment worn over armor

 wallow: to lie down and roll around in something, or devote oneself entirely to something

Visit the carolemarshmysteries.com website to:

- Join the Carole Marsh Mysteries™ Fan Club!

- Write a letter to Christina, Grant, Mimi, or Papa!

- Cast your vote for where the next mystery should take place!

- Find fascinating facts about the countries where the mysteries take place!

- Track your reading on an international map!

- Take the Fact or Fiction online quiz!

- Play the Around-the-World Scavenger Hunt computer game!

- Find out where the *Mystery Girl* is flying next!